A Tale of
Paradise City

A Novella

Written by Donna Fox

For My Husband,

Because love will always find a way.

With love,
D.F.

Foreward:

The idea for this novella came from the cover photo, after a friend suggested I try drawing inspiration from pictures I have taken. Which is a very loose translation of an ekphrastic.

Happy Reading,
D.F.

Chapter One:

A warm breeze trickled through the bars, carrying the sweet scent emanating from pink flowers sprouting from vines that strangled the wrought-iron bars. Which separated the Outer Ring from the Inner Circle of Paradise City.

Paula breathed in the sweet floral scent with closed eyes as she absorbed the warm rays of sunlight that danced through the bars and left little freckled kisses on her pale skin. She pressed her forehead against the wrought-iron bars and embraced the coolness of the Inner Circle's side on her skin. Slowly. She opened her eyes, her gaze fell longingly upon the marketplace below as she wrapped her fingers around the bars and pulled herself closer, yet.

"You act like there isn't sunlight on this side of the wall," Marco chortled from alongside her. He remained in the shade of the protective stone wall. His sky-blue eyes watched her with adoration.

"They say we're the ones of privilege, we have the freedom to do as we please. But we can't leave this place, even if that's what we desire." Paula replied as she opened her eyes to admire her favourite view of Paradise City and the surrounding land.
Her sand-coloured eyes traced the peaks of the mountains that served as a backdrop to the business of the Outer Ring.

The same breeze that carried the scent of those pink flowers wound its way through the city and rustled the leaves of palm trees that grew among the stone homes beyond the market.

"It's safe here, Paula." Marco muttered as she stepped into the sunlight alongside her and leaned a shoulder against the bars. He furrowed his brow as he studied her with curiosity.

"That's what I keep hearing." She murmured, then closed her eyes again as she let herself get lost in the sounds of the marketplace below.

"Just look at them," Marco expressed with an air of repulsion in his voice. "Everyone is dirty and barely scraping by to survive. Up here, we want for nothing and have the protection of the guards to keep us safe. Why would we even want to venture out there when we have everything we could ever want within these walls?" He asked, his lips pinched together as he wrinkled his nose in distaste.

"You just don't get it, Marco." Paula sighed with contempt. She opened her eyes again and continued to admire the business of the marketplace.
She watched families with small children navigate the crowds, salesmen lead their livestock in search of a buyer, merchants haggle with customers, and so on.

"Then explain it to me." Marco requested, his sky-blue eyes watched her with curiosity.

She turned and met his gaze before she allowed herself to examine the more subtle features of his face. The faded cluster of freckles that danced across his upper cheeks and nose, the squareness of his jawline, the hazel centres of his sky-blue eyes. The creases that formed in the corners of his eyes when he smiled at her.

"Not today, Marco." She sighed with a smile and pushed herself away from the bars.

"Then let's finish our walk," he murmured as he reached out and pushed her raven-coloured hair away from her face. He gently tucked a few strands behind her ear and took in her round face appraisingly.

"As you wish." She mumbled. Then allowed Marco to take her by the hand and lead her onward.

They walked along the wall until they reached the Inner Circle's marketplace. Just beside the only gate that led to the Outer Ring, for those with permits.

The Inner Circle's marketplace was a lot tamer than the Outer Ring's. The merchants didn't barter with the customers, and there were copious amounts of personal space for one to meander at their leisure.

"They get to come and go as they like. Sell the same goods every day with no bartering or competition for the products. They're just here to provide for us. Why even have them sell us the products at all?" Paula wondered aloud, as they walked right down the middle of the walkway and everyone moved aside for them.

"Because we can't ask them to provide us with these products for nothing. That's practically stealing," Marco explained, then pulled her closer and offered an arm for her to take.

She accepted and they continued onward. "I'm not saying for free. Just that there isn't much variety or competition to sell the products. I'm left wondering what draws the merchants to continue to sell to us when the price is always the same. There's no chance of them making anything extra." She explained as they sauntered through the crowd.

"That would be complete chaos and we wouldn't be able to guarantee the merchants their allotted amounts. Nor our people the products they depend on." He dismissed with a sigh of impatience.
Then, he suddenly put on a faux smile as a councilman approached, and they were forced to pause this conversation.

They stood for a few minutes and chatted with the man about political views and new bills soon-to-be passed.

Paula smiled politely but paid minimal attention as she pondered life outside the wall.

"Well, I best let you get the future missus home before sundown. The nights are getting chilly with the autumn months approaching." The man stated with a tight smile pulled across his wrinkled face.

This roused Paula from her reverie. She gave another polite smile and nodded in farewell.

"Thank you, councilman." Marco nodded, and they continued on their way.
He waited until they were out of earshot. "Still dreaming of a different life?" He leaned down and his warm breath tickled her neck just below the ear.

She nodded and turned her sandy gaze to raise a brow in curiosity.

"Don't you ever wonder what life is like beyond the gates of the Inner Circle?" She queried with a playful smile on her blush pink lips.

"I don't," he stated, with an amused smile playing at the corners of his lips, "because I'm grateful for what I've been given." He shot her a pointed look.

"I suppose curiosity is my curse to bear, then," Paula mumbled to herself as she pushed her lips to the side in a disappointed grimace.

"And you bear it so well," He crooned, then leaned in and placed a kiss on her temple. "Now, I need to go help Mother with a few things. Be careful in your wanderings and I'll see you at dinner?" He asked as he released her from his grasp.

She nodded in agreement with a smile of appreciation.

Then watched him disappear into the crowd, or as much as he could, when people stepped aside to create a path for him.

Paula wandered in the opposite direction until she emerged out the other side of the market, which was about to close for the night. She followed the stone wall at the backside until she got to the gate where she watched the parade of merchants as they left for the day.
A large cart of produce rolled by and she let her intrusive thoughts win as she jumped into the back. She hoped to hide amongst the barrels of fruit and vegetables until they passed through the gate. Only to have her hopes dashed as the cart came to a stop.
Followed by the sound of boots as they shuffled along the cobblestone road.

"Paula, we've talked about this." The voice of Helmar called from just beyond the barrel.

With a sigh, she rose from her hiding place and accepted his hand to help her climb out.
"It was worth a try." She mumbled as Helmar waved the driver off and they stepped to the side to let other merchants pass.

"You'll have to do better than that to get by me." He stated as he wore a smile of amusement but still watched the merchants that filed out of the gates.

"I just wanted to wander the Outer Ring's market for a few minutes and then I was coming right back. I swear." Paula simpered as she crossed her arms in a pout and watched the gates close behind the last merchant.

"Marco would kill me if I even thought of allowing that," Helmar stated with a look of pity in his nearly black eyes.

"Right." She agreed and deflated in further disappointment.

"It's almost supper time. You should head to Miss Marissa's house before they come looking for you." He suggested and grunted to clear his throat in discomfort.

"You're right. Thanks, Helm." Paula bid him and paced away, headed for her future mother-in-law's home.

Chapter Two:

Paula supervised the servants as they set the table and arranged the dining room for dinner.

"Paula, dear. Sit down, please, you'll overwork yourself." Marissa, Marco's mother, requested as she took a seat and patted the chair beside her.

Paula sat beside her with a strained smile.

A servant ran over to pour them each a glass of wine and she accepted it with a more sincere smile in thanks.

"You two are such a wonderful match." Marissa began, "In only a few short months, we will start planning your wedding. It will be the biggest celebration Paradise City has had in years." She hummed as her sky-blue eyes glowed with hungry anticipation.

"Remind me why we must continue to wait, even though we've known about the match for as long as I can remember?" Paula questioned as she sipped her wine.

"Because, dear, it would be tacky to plan the wedding before you two are officially engaged." She explained and rolled her eyes in annoyance.

"Right," Paula agreed with a nod and then took a longer drink of her wine as she waited for the discomfort to pass.

The rest of dinner revolved around bland topics such as the weather and politics, but was accompanied it with much more wine.

Paula was all too grateful when Marco suggested they take an evening stroll afterwards.

The streets of the Inner Circle were empty as the pair of them walked together, their arms linked at the elbow. Rich moonlight bathed the cobblestone as they carried on through the silent streets until they found themselves at Paula's favourite lookout.

She wrapped her hands around the bars as she peered down at the marketplace.

It was a lot more peaceful now than it was this afternoon. The sea of bodies dwindled to just a handful of people who still milled about in the cool night air.

She observed through the bars in curiosity, getting caught up in the stories she imagined for the people she watched every day. Things like how many children they had, what their homes looked like, and what their way of life might be like.

"What are you thinking about?" Marco muttered as he reached out and brushed a few strands of her raven hair out of her eyes. His sky-blue gaze appraised her with a tender expression of adoration.

She sighed. "I was just thinking about Amman and his family. I was thinking how hard it must be for him to work late, instead of being home with his wife and kids at dinnertime," Paula replied as she watched the merchant in the fabric stall pack up his things.

"You know him?" Marco asked with a furrowed brow in confusion.

"No," Paula stated and then met his gaze. "I just feel like I do because I watch them so much. Sometimes I make up stories or things about them, so I feel like I'm a part of that world." She explained with a shrug and returned her gaze to the near-empty marketplace.

A small smile formed across his lips as he observed her.

The moonlight illuminated her once beige-coloured skin and gave it a silvery sheen. Her sand-brown eyes shimmered as she watched the last of the market's occupants leave for the night.

"Your imagination and curious mind have always been what's fascinated me about you. It's what drew me to you." He spoke in a low murmur, his eyes sparkled as he continued to appraise her.

Paula turned her gaze upon him, drawn in by his words.

"I still remember the day I first saw you, playing outside that hovel your family called home. The servants carried our caravan through the streets. Your raven-coloured hair was a mess as it threatened to fall out of the braid your mother wove it in. Your clothes were falling apart and filthy with grime. But then you looked up at me with those magical eyes of yours and I was hooked." He stated with a fond smile. His eyes carried a distant gaze in reflection.

"I'd hounded my mother the rest of the ride to go back so that we could find you." Marco began again, then bit his lips together in thought.

"A few days later, they'd brought you to our private courtyard to play with me, after you'd been fed and cleaned up. It was then that I was certain this was a match made in heaven." He finished and reached out to cradle her cheeks in his hands. Then leaned in to place a soft kiss on her forehead.

Paula accepted the kiss, but her mind wandered as she fought the curiosity of what life might have been like if she stayed in the Outer Ring.

She tried to fight the words that burst from her lips.

"I wonder if my parents objected to me being taken." She murmured as Marco released her face and she scanned the homes of the Outer Ring, beyond the marketplace.

"They received generous payment and life became easier without the worry of feeding you. Plus, you got to move to a life of luxury in the Inner Circle. That's an opportunity most would kill for," Marco replied his expression stricken and slightly stiff.

"I'm just glad I could convince my mother that you were worth saving." He added, and a relieved smile broke across his lips.

"Thank you," Paula replied in a hollow voice. She knew it was what Marco wanted to hear.

With his free hand, Marco grasped one of the pink flowers on the vines that wrapped around the bars. He plucked and tucked it in Paula's hair behind her ear. Then, using the tips of his fingers, he lifted her chin to better appraise the flower's placement.

She allowed it and did her best not to let the mask of contentment slip under Marco's careful eye.

"We should turn in for the night," He stated and pulled his hand away from her chin to offer his arm in guidance.

Paula wrapped her arms around his and allowed him to lead the way to their shared courtyard. Where they bid each other good night and parted ways to their separate dwellings.
Once she closed the door behind herself, Paula leaned against it and let out a deep sigh. She closed her eyes and lifted her chin to the sky in reprieve as she stood there for a moment and absorbed the silence of her home.
With another sigh, she opened her eyes, crossed the room, and poured herself a glass of wine. Then made her way to her barred bedroom window that overlooked the nicest of the Outer Ring's neighbourhoods. She sipped her wine and watched as the candlelit windows blinked out, one by one, until only the moon's glow shone on the sleepy city. Which was her cue to turn in for the night because she had another full day of wearing her mask of gratitude, on its way.

Chapter Three:

Paula's dressing maids awakened her the next morning. They catered to her every need as the sun crested over the horizon. Then took her to meet Marco for breakfast.

"Good morning, Paula. You look elegant in that gown of gold and cerulean blue." Marco greeted her as he stood to pull her chair out, then tucked her in. His sky-blue eyes twinkled with delight as he took the seat across from her.

"Why thank you, Marco. I know your mother says gold is flattering on everyone, but I would argue that cerulean blue is too." She commented with a soft smile.

"I would have to agree," he stated and continued to watch her in adoration.

"What's on the agenda today?" Paula inquired as she dished up their food.

"I have a few meetings that I must attend, but after that, I'm all yours," Marco answered with a playful wink as he took his first bite of breakfast.

"I suppose I can entertain myself for the time being." Paula teased with a smirk, her sandy brown eyes twinkled coyly.

They laughed together as they finished their breakfast before parting ways for the morning.

....

Paula wandered the market and many public gardens within the Inner Circle. She watched families on their morning outings and young couples as they enjoyed the sunshine.
Somehow, the intricacies of life in the Inner Circle weren't as enticing as the lives Paula imagined in the Outer Ring. So it wasn't a shock when her feet carried her to her favourite viewpoint, where she overlooked their marketplace from behind the wrought-iron bars of a terrace that sat above them.

"I thought I'd find you here." Marco's gentle voice pulled Paula's gaze from the chaotic street below.

"Here I am," she muttered with a weak smile and returned her gaze to the marketplace.

"Still longing for things beyond your reach?" He inquired, his head tilted in interest. Marco's sky-blue eyes held a look of pity as his brows pinched together in thought.

"Today, I've been wondering what my life might have been like if I was still out there." She murmured, her sand-coloured eyes tracked a mother and her two children as they wove through the crowd.

"I think you forget how lucky you are to be chosen. How lucky you are to be saved from that miserable existence." Marco's voice deepened and drew Paula's gaze back to him. His eyes darkened in disappointment as he frowned down at her and his lips pursed together in a pout.

"I think you should run along and meet Mother for lunch. I'll be there shortly." He commanded with a flare of his nostrils.

"Yes, sir," Paula agreed and was on her way to Marissa's.

....

Even the clatter of the plates being cleared from the table couldn't drown out Marissa's shrill voice as she droned on about the same subject for over an hour and a half.

"You, of all people, know how dangerous it is outside the wall. I know you were young, but surely you remember some of your time from the Outer Ring. Even the smallest of details should be enough to make you want to stay here, instead of returning to that wretched place." Marissa rambled and only stopped to take a long sip of wine that now stained the edges of her lips.

"Mother, it's an afternoon outing. Nothing will happen. We will be in and out before an hour is up. So please, just enjoy your wine and let me do something nice for my future fiancé." Marco finally intervened with a warning glare at his mother.

"Something nice would be surprising her with jewellery. Not stuffing her into a hot tent with a guarded escort. Never mind the unsavoury tour of a part of our city that's best forgotten." She scoffed and slurped down the last of her wine, then thrust the empty glass into the air in demand of a refill.

"I'll talk to you about this later," Marco growled as he got to his feet. "Come, Paula, our palanquin awaits." He added as he continued to glare at his mother and held out his arm to escort Paula from his mother's dwelling.

....

Moments later, they arrived at the gates where their palanquin and guarded escort awaited. Marco and Paula got inside, then the bearers lifted them onto their shoulders and carried them out of the Inner Circle.

A foul smell wafted through the curtains of their palanquin as they passed through the gates into the Outer Ring.

"What is that?" Paula gasped as the gates closed behind them. She lifted her scarf to her nose and her lips turned downward in disgust.

"It must be street sweeping day," Marco commented with a nod of approval. "The smell is much better than usual." He added with a fond smile as he reached over and placed a gentle hand on her ankle.

"How fortunate," she replied as her eyes watered and she fought the urge to gag.

Suddenly, the palanquin bearers paused as a group of haggard people charged and the guards created a perimeter to protect them.

"What's happening now?" Pauls asked as she leaned closer to Marco in fear.

"Just beggars. The guards will handle them." He stated with a dismissive wave and bored expression.

A solid thud cracked through the air, followed by the crowd quickly dispersing.

The guards moved back to their previous formation and revealed the body of someone lying unconscious on the ground.

Before Paula could get a look, the palanquin bearers moved forward, and carried them over the motionless body. She glanced backwards at the body until their palanquin rounded a corner.

The bearers carried them along the exterior wall until it got to the Outer Ring's market, where a whole new smell wafted through the curtains.

Paula clamped her hand over her face in disgust, and her lunch turned in her stomach.

"Ah, fresh fish day. How luck for us." Marco hummed with a smile as he gave Paula a sideways glance in amusement.

She didn't bother to respond as she realized he was doing all of this to mock her curiosity and deter her from further exploration.

The caravan veered away from the wall and headed down a side street.

"Where are we going now?" Paula asked, as she curiously leaned closer to the curtain and tried to peer at the homes they passed.

"We're almost there." Marco replied with a soft smile. His sky-blue eyes teased her with a secret only he knew, and she was about to find out.

Then the caravan stopped, and their palanquin was lowered so that they could exit.

"Come." He beckoned as he crawled out and offered a hand to help her.

Paula's breath hitched in her throat as she pushed the curtains aside and laid eyes on a fully decimated home. There was a pang of recognition in the back of her mind as she stood alongside Marco and took in the devastation before her.

The home's intricate brickwork was now reduced to rubble.

"This was your home before we rescued you." He explained. His sky-blue eyes held pity and his lips turned down in an uncomfortable grimace.

"What happened?" Paula whispered as she clutched at her chest in shock.

"Honestly, we don't know." He began in a solemn voice as they walked closer to the wreckage and he wrapped an arm around her. "One day, our messenger came to deliver our monthly dowery and found this," He explained with a lacklustre shrug.

"Why are you showing me this?" She asked, her brows pinched together in anguish.

"I needed you to see how dangerous the Outer Ring is and that you have nothing left to go back to." He mumbled shamefully.

Suddenly, a loud hiss filled the air, followed by a deafening bang. Fire exploded all around them and black smoke blinded Paula as chaos broke out in the aftermath.

Confusion and fear filled her mind as she watched the bodies scatter, unable to hear anything but muffled cries and a ringing in her ears. Then another explosion erupted, and she fell into the blackness of unconsciousness.

Chapter Four:

With a groan, Paula pushed herself up from the dirt she laid in. Her head throbbed with unbearable pain as she automatically touched her temple and found a slick red ichor that made her stomach turn.

"Hey, there's someone over there." A young man's voice called out.

Paula's vision blurred as she turned and the figure approached with the crunch of gravelly-dirt under foot.

"Paula?" The same voice muttered with uncertainty as she fell unconscious once more.

....

Paula groaned again as she opened her eyes to a dimly lit stone-walled room. She moaned as her head pounded in pain, and fought to sit up, every inch of her body felt stiff and sore.

"Easy there, you have quite the bump on your head." A gentle but rich voice murmured. The same one she'd heard before she passed out in the street.

"Where am I?" Paula mumbled. Her hand reached for her temple again, and found a bandage that covered her wound. It was tender to the touch, but felt better than when she'd first woken up. Her brain felt hazy, and it was hard to focus her gaze on anything, but the dirt floor beneath her.

"You're-"

"Enos, what did you do?" boomed another male voice.

"Shit, just give me a second." Enos, the owner of the familiar male's voice, mumbled. Followed by the shuffle of him jumping to his feet in a panic.
"Look Liam, she-"

"I don't want to hear it. When they come looking for her and arrest us because they think we attacked the Senator to kidnap her. That's on you!" The second male's voice scolded. He stood just beyond the threshold of the room Paula sat in.

"Listen, she needed help and he just left her-"

"No. I don't want to hear any of this. I'm going for a drink, and you need to get rid of her, before someone finds out she's here." Liam stated then shuffled away.

With a sigh, Enos turned back to Paula and sank to his knees.
"I'm sorry about him." He apologized with a thumb pointed over his shoulder.
"He's just jumpy after the attack the rebels executed on you and your fiancé." He explained. Enos' sage-green eyes appraised her carefully, his pale lips pulled tight with unease.

"He's not my fiancé." Paula corrected with an exhausted sigh. She squeezed her eyes shut as the pounding in her head intensified.

"Oh, sorry. I thought-"

"We're waiting until I'm of age before he asks me."
She explained with a huff of exhaustion.

For a second, he blinked at her in confusion but
shook it off.
"Here, have some water." Enos offered and lifted a
cup to her mouth.

As the water passed her lips, she felt a mixture of
relief and disgust at the muddy taste.
"Thank you," she spoke through puckered lips.

"What's your name?" Enos asked as he placed the
cup down. He watched her in anticipation as though
he already knew the answer.

Momentarily, Paula got lost in his sage-green gaze.
She spotted little chocolate brown flecks that were
spread throughout.
"Paula," she mumbled in a barely audible voice and
cleared her throat nervously as she pulled her gaze
away from his.

He offered her more water, but she held a hand up to
decline.
"I'm sure it tastes like crap, but this is all I have, and
you need to stay hydrated." Enos expressed and ran
a hand through his chin-length onyx black hair,
before he offered it to her again.

With a nod, she accepted the cup and drained it in
several gulps. A grainy sensation remained on her
tongue long after she had finished. But the water
had taken away some of the haziness from her tired
and sore brain.

"Thank you." She mumbled again, "How did I get here?" She asked, and her gaze wandered about the small room.

"I found you in the street after the attack and brought you here." He explained as he bit his lips together in unease. Then brushed his long dark hair out of his face, again.

"Thank you for taking care of me, but I should head home now. I'm sure Marco will be worried about me." She stated and attempted to get up.

"I think you should rest for the night. Besides, the streets aren't safe right now," Enos countered. He held his hands out, prepared to push her back onto the makeshift bed.

"But-"

"Trust me." He begged, his green eyes wide in pleading.

"Okay." Paula nodded and was immediately dizzy from the motion. With a sigh, she rubbed her eyes in exhaustion. "I can barely remember what happened. I remember two explosions and then waking up here." She stated. Her headache pulsed in her temple as she tried to recall more.

"Your palanquin and guarded escort was attacked by some rebels who were after your boyfriend. You got caught in the crossfire." He explained with a nervous gulp.

"What happened to him?" She asked. A lump of fear formed in her throat.

"He got away." Enos' eyes darkened in an unreadable expression.

She sighed in relief. "Good, I was scared he was still out there, or worse. Dead." She replied, and the lump in her throat dissolved in reprieve.

"Right." Enos agreed with a tentative nod. His eyes fixed on hers with a look of trepidation. "Anyway, why don't we get some rest and we can get you back home tomorrow?" He offered, his lips pulled tight in a grimace.

"Okay. Thank you, Enos." Paula mumbled as she lay down, and he blew out the single candle that lit the room.

Chapter Five:

The following morning, a stream of sunlight spilled through the window and woke Paula as it cascaded over her eyes. It took her a moment to re-familiarize herself with the surroundings of Enos' home.

"Good morning." He greeted her with a broad smile and approached with a tray of food. "How does your head feel?" He asked, his sage-green eyes appraised her with concern.

"Much better, thank you," Paula replied with a slight groan as she sat up. Her back felt stiff from sleeping on the floor.

"Here, have something to eat," Enos offered, as he set the tray on the floor, between them.

"Oh no, I couldn't." She tried to decline as she thought of the muddy water from the previous night.

"Just have a little something to hold you over until you get home." He insisted and pushed the tray closer.

Reluctantly, she accepted a piece of flatbread and took a small bite of it. The dryness absorbed what little saliva she had in her mouth, which left her chewing it for longer than desirable. Begrudgingly, she picked up the cup in front of her, as she brought

it to her lips. The scent of warm spices swirled up in the form of steam and kissed her upper lip.
"What is this?" She asked, as she inhaled the smell again and it settled in her chest as though it clung to her soul. "It smells wonderful." Her sandy-coloured eyes lit up with delight.

"Tea." He replied with a furrowed brow in intrigue.

"Oh," she sighed in disappointment. "I'm not allowed to have tea." She stated and set the cup down, her lips turned downward in discontent.

"What?" Enos asked as an amused smile crept across his lips.

"Miss Marissa says ladies don't drink caffeine." She explained in a rehearsed voice but pushed her lips to the side in regret.

He scoffed. "Have you ever tried tea?" He asked, his sage green eyes twinkling at her with curiosity.

Paula shook her head as her eyes flickered to the caramel-coloured liquid on the tray.

He grabbed the cup and brought it to his lips, all the while Paula tracked it in envy.
"How long have you been with Marco's family?" He inquired, his eyes narrowed in interest as he took a long, loud slurp of the tea.

Her mouth watered enviously. "Since I was quite young. I don't remember my life before I lived with them. But if I had to guess, I've lived with them for at least the last ten or twelve years." She sighed and tracked the cup as Enos set it down on the tray between them. Then licked her lips in lust as she eyed the delicious-smelling elixir known as tea.

"You'll be going back today and likely won't get the chance to try it ever again." He suggested, his eyes alight with enjoyment as he toyed with her.

"Right." She sighed and deflated further at the realization.

"So, maybe you should try it now?" He offered with a smile as he held it out to her.

"Oh no. I shouldn't." She shook her head vigorously in denial.

"Just a sip." He coerced and leaned across the tray with it outstretched to her. The smell wafted in her direction.

Paula licked her lips once more, then her eyes fell on the liquid within the glass.
"One sip can't hurt, right?" She asked, her leery gaze fell on Enos.

"It'll be our little secret." He replied with a playful wink.

She nodded in agreement and accepted the cup. Then tentatively brought the warm liquid to her lips. She blew on it nervously and the steam curled around her nostrils again. Paula felt engulfed by the delightful smell as it wrapped her soul in a warm hug.
Then, with the smallest of sips, she allowed the caramel liquid to pass over her lips and further drench her soul in placidity.
"Oh, my," was all she could say as she held the cup close to her chest, languishing the warmth of it.
Paula closed her eyes and breathed deeply to take in this wondrous liquid's scent more deeply.

She opened her eyes to find Enos with his hand held out in expectation, and she reluctantly handed it over. The corners of her mouth turned down in sadness, knowing she could never enjoy the tea's embrace again.

Enos chuckled, and his eyes lit up in adoration. "Do you want to finish the cup? I can always pour another for myself." He held it out to her once more.

"I suppose," she agreed. "As long as you don't mind." She added as an after thought and accepted the cup once more.

"Not at all." He replied with a kind smile as he continued to steal peaks of her in her blissful moment.

The rest of breakfast was quiet as Paula enjoyed her tea and Enos ate what remained on the tray.

She helped him clean up, and then the pair of them made their way to the Inner Circle's gates.
"Thank you for everything," Paula hummed as they stood against the stone wall, "I-"

"Forget it. I'm just happy to have gotten you home safely." He dismissed with a wave and slowly backed away. "I hope you have a good rest of your life. Stay safe, will you?" He bid her with a wry smile and disappeared into the crowded street.

With a sigh, Paula walked up the ramp to the gates.

"Halt." The guard at the entrance called. "Do you have a permit?" He inquired, his dark eyes narrowed in suspicion.

"I live here," Paula stated in a small voice of appreciation.

"I'm sure." The guard replied as his doubtful eyes glanced at her haggard appearance.

She followed his gaze and realized what she must look like, having not bathed or removed the bandage on her head since the attack. "I'm Marco's future fiancé, Paula." She tried to explain as she pulled the bandage off and her lower lip quivered in fear.

"Impossible. She died in the rebel attack yesterday. Go back to your hovel, wench." The guard growled and shoved her away.

Paula skittered down the ramp and looked back at the guard. She wore an expression of anguish and confusion. Then stood there for a long moment, unsure of what to do next.
It made sense to her that if Marco returned on his own, they would assume she was dead, but it hadn't even been a full day since their trip.
The fact that there wasn't a search party out for her and that Marco had given up on her already, didn't sit well with Paula. She was at a loss for how she could prove her identity or, better yet, show Marco she was okay.
Until she remembered that her favourite view of the Outer Ring's market was a fond pastime of his as well. She just hoped that he'd be there today and maybe she'd be fortunate enough to get his attention. Surely he'd be relieved to see she was alive and welcome her back with open arms. All she had to do was navigate her way back there.

Chapter Six:

Paula found her way to the chaotic Outer Ring's market, and it was a lot more boisterous than she thought it would be. The crowd was hard to weave through, but she managed it as she kept her sights set on the wrought iron-barred window above. As she got closer, she could make out the form of Marco as he leaned against the bars and observed the sea of bodies she swam through.

His brows were pinched together in thought as he scanned the crowd with his sky-blue eyes.

Paula's heart stopped for a moment as she laid eyes on him and sighed in relief. She did her best to stand her ground and remain in the middle of the crowd. She waved her hands wildly to get his attention. "Marco!" She called on repeat. Which made the people around her give her a wide berth as they passed by. She watched his eyes as they seemed to meet hers in a moment of recognition, but he shook his head in disbelief and turned in another direction.

"Paula?" A familiar voice drew her attention.

"Enos?" she asked in shock.

"What are you doing here?" He asked, his brow furrowed in confusion as his sage green eyes searched her for an answer.

"They wouldn't let me back in. They said Marco told them I was dead. So now I'm trying to get his attention in hopes of being let me back in." She explained with a point toward Marco, who remained in place, just above them.

He followed her point with a curious gaze and then spotted their target.
"Come with me, I don't think he can see you here," Enos stated, then took her by the hand and led her to the fabric merchant. There he bargained a few coins to borrow a roll of red fabric so that they could use it as a flag while Paula stood on top of his stall.

The merchant agreed, mostly because he was friends with Enos.

She called Marco until his eyes landed on her and a hint of recognition flashed through them.

His jaw dropped, and he slowly backed away from the bars with a terrified expression on his face.

"I think he saw me," Paula stated as she jumped down from the workbench and handed back the roll of cloth to the merchant. "Thank you so much for your help. I wish I had something to offer to repay you." She sighed and turned her lips downward in regret.

"That bracelet of yours is pretty. My wife would love one like it." The merchant commented with a thoughtful smile.

"Of course," Paula agreed, "Oh, and have the matching earrings." She offered as she placed them into his open palm, as well.

"Thank you, my lady." He spoke in appreciation with a nod of respect.

"No, thank you, sir." She replied, then grabbed Enos' hand and led him back through the crowd toward the gates.

"Where are we going?" He asked as he allowed her to pull him.

"He saw me and I'm sure he's waiting at the gates for me." She explained as they jogged along.

Sure enough, there stood Marco as he talked to one of the guards.

"Thank you again for your help." She spoke with a grateful smile, then wrapped Enos in a hug and headed up the ramp.

But this time Enos hung around to watch what followed.

An excited Paula ran up to where Marco and the guard were in deep conversation.
Unable to contain herself, "I'm sorry it took me so long to get home." She muttered, her voice hoarse from shouting to get his attention.

The two men paused and looked at her like a cockroach that had just crawled out from under the cupboard.

"Do you know this woman?" The guard asked Marco with a furrowed brow in disgust.

Marco's eyes met Paula's as he shook his head and looked back at the guard. "I do not." He muttered and pinched his lips together in a pout of disgust.

"It's me, Paula." She mumbled in a barely audible voice as a tightness formed in her chest.

"The Senator's future fiancé died. You are mistaken." The guard growled as he glared at Paula, whose eyes stared into Marco's. "I thought I told you not to come back here, wench? Be gone before I make you regret it." The guard gave her another forceful shove while Marco stood by and watched.

Tears ran down Paula's cheeks as she stood halfway up the ramp. She stared at Marco in shock and hurt as her heart broke in that moment.

"It's time to go, Paula," Enos stated as he wrapped an arm around her shoulders and steered her away.

"But he's right there." She pleaded, "He said he doesn't know me." She explained as her lower lip trembled and she tried to hold back the tears that spilled from her eyes.

"Let's go somewhere quiet, so I can explain this to you." He offered in a low mumble.

"Do you think he doesn't recognize me?" She questioned as she glanced back at the gates, where Marco had been moments ago.

"No, I think he recognizes you. But let's have this conversation elsewhere." He requested as he continued to guide her along.

"Then why won't he help me?" She spat and a fire burned in her watery eyes.

"He doesn't want to, Paula. In the aftermath of the attack, I watched him abandon you. He saw you lying there and just took off without you." Enos explained in a barely audible voice, his sage green eyes narrowed with pity.

"That's not true," she argued and tossed another hopeful glance over her shoulder.

"Paula-"

"No, you just don't want me to be happy. You'd rather I stayed here instead of returning to the Inner Circle." She accused as she shrugged him off.

"You weren't happy there to begin with." He argued, his eyes smouldered at her in accusation.

Paula paused in shock, her lower lip still trembled but her eyes were wide as she stared at Enos in disbelief. Then, with the snap of a finger, she took off through the busy streets of Paradise City. Tears continued to spill from her eyes as she blindly ran until she found an abandoned street far away from the busy crowd.
Paula panted as her feet came to a halt and she slammed her shoulder against the nearest wall. Then slid down it and she fell to her knees. Anguish encompassed her body and squeezed her chest as she shamelessly wept into her cupped hands.
She remained this way until a set of footsteps approached and someone knelt beside her.

"Paula?" Enos whispered as he placed a gentle hand on her shoulder.

She aggressively wiped away the last few tears but refused to look at him. Paula stared at the ground as she clenched her jaw in anger.

"I'm sorry this is happening to you." He mumbled and settled himself down in the dirt alongside her.

Paula pursed her lips together to fight the urge to tell him to go away.

"When I was young, I had this neighbour, a girl, that I would play with every day. She and I would go on adventures, terrorizing the merchants in the market and stirring up all kinds of trouble." He began as his hand moved to Paula's back and rubbed it soothingly. "She and I did everything together, as did our families. I'd always thought that we'd grow up and marry one day. But then the Inner Circle's guards came and took her from her us. They even destroyed her home with the rest of her family inside it, as a warning to anyone who wanted to come looking for her." He sighed in thought as his gaze stared at the dirt beneath their feet.

"What happened to her?" Paula asked. She watched him in apprehension.

"We never heard from her again. But now, as an adult, I have joined the Outer Ring's rebels as a way of seeking justice for my friend and her family." He replied with an extra long sigh of disappointment.

"Why are you telling me this?" She inquired, her brow furrowed in curiosity.

"Because I'm on your side, even if you don't believe me. I want you to know that I'm here for you and I know what you're going through. I know what it's like to lose the life you expected to live." He explained, a fire burned in his eyes as he spoke.

"Thank you." Was all she could say as she looked into his sage green eyes and felt grateful to have him at her side in this moment of need.

"Come with me." He requested and pulled her to stand beside him.

"Where are we going?" Paula asked. She almost feared the determination in his gaze.

"To find Liam," Enos replied and continued to hold her hand as he led her along.

Chapter Seven:

Paula and Enos stood in front of a loud, busy building with far too many people inside.

"What is this place?" She asked in a small voice, her eyes wide in fear as she watched a man empty his stomach through an open window. Her feet turned to stone instantly and her stomach turned itself into nauseous knots in response.

"Right." Enos sighed, with a forgetful tap on his forehead.
"I'm sorry, Paula." He apologized and backtracked to stand beside her. "This is a tavern. You can get food and drink here." He explained with a gesture toward the chaos that spilled out of the building's doors and windows.

Paula didn't have a response as she stood in paralysis and watched the scene before her in disgust.

"I know it's intimidating. We're only going in to find Liam and then coming straight out." He explained and bit his lips together nervously. His gaze darted between the tavern and Paula with unease.
"Or I could go while you wait here?" He offered, his brow cocked upward in suggestion.

"No, I'm staying with you." She objected and grabbed his hand in hers. With a nervous swallow. "Let's go." she sighed as she hardened her gaze in focus.

"Okay, we'll make this quick." He stated. Then squeezed her hand in reassurance and led the way.

Linked by their joined hands, Enos wove through the crowd at the door and pulled Paula along.

It was even louder than Paula expected inside, but the noise was nothing compared to the smell. Urine mixed with yeast, body odour, and various other unidentifiable smells.

Enos led her up to the bar and flagged down the barkeep. "Have you seen Liam?" He shouted over the ruckus around them.

"I give nothing away for free." The barkeep stated with a grumpy snarl.

"Fine," Enos agreed with an annoyed eye roll. He dug into his pocket and produced a few coins. "An ale then." He huffed and placed the coins in the barkeep's open hand.

"For you and your friend," He snapped and slapped his open hand back down in expectation.

"She doesn't need one." Enos tried to protest.

"Then she doesn't need to be in here." The barkeep countered and gave an innocent shrug.

"Fine, one each." He agreed and placed more coins in the man's grubby hand.

The barkeep accepted the coins and turned around as he prepared something Paula couldn't see.

"You ever have an ale before?" Enos murmured in a barely audible voice as the barkeep returned and presented them with two mugs overflowing with a frothy golden liquid.

Paula shook her head, her sandy eyes wide in apprehension as she peered into the mug. At least she understood where the prevalent smell of yeast came from.

"So, where is he?" Enos snapped at the barkeep as he tried to slink away.

"Oh, he's in the corner with his buddies." The man answered with a nod in Liam's direction.

"Thanks," Enos replied. Then grabbed his ale and looked at Paula in expectation.
His gaze flicked between her and the mug of ale on the bar top, then he looked at his hand that held hers as though weighing his options.

She furrowed her brow in confusion, and then the realization hit her.
"You're not letting go of my hand." She stated and scooped up the mug before he could second guess her.

"Are you sure?" He asked, his sage green eyes danced in amusement.

"Certain. Now, let's find Liam." She added with a nod as some of the ale sloshed onto the floor.

"Braun hates when we spill everywhere. Take a couple of sips of your ale to make it easier to carry."

He instructed and brought his mug to his lips, then slurped it too loud to be polite.

She watched him with a frown of disapproval as her eyes darted between Enos and her mug.

"What?" He asked, using his sleeve to wipe away the foam that sat on his upper lip. "It's good, I swear. Much better than the water, I can assure you." He added with a playful wink and half smile in amusement to see her hesitation.

Nervously, she brought the mug to her lips and prayed he was right. As she took a sip the wheat-flavoured liquid spilled over her tongue and down her gullet with surprising ease. She licked her lips to clear the foam from the edges and looked up at Enos in thought.

"What do you think?" He asked, his eyes twinkling with curiosity.

A smile crept across her face and Paula nodded in approval before she brought it to her lips again for another sip.

"Okay, that's enough. I still need you to be standing by the time we leave." He chuckled.

Paula pulled the mug away and peered inside. She'd drained more of the ale from it than she'd realized. "Let's find Liam," she agreed as a heat rose in her cheeks.

Enos nodded in approval and led the way.

Again, they wove through a sea of bodies until there was a gap. They'd emerged and at a nearby table sat Liam with several other men, all of which wore expressions of cheer as they laughed and conversed loudly.

"Liam!" Enos called as they approached.

"Eh! Glad you could make it." He beamed at Enos until his eyes landed on Paula and his expression fell. He muttered something to his companions with a fake smile, then intercepted Paula and Enos before they reached the table.
"What is she doing here?" He scolded Enos with a fatherly scowl.

"She-"

"Do you know what people will think if they realize she's the missing girl from the Inner Circle?" He questioned and shot Paula a look of disgust.

"She's not-"

"What if they discover her with you and think that you attacked the Senator so that you could kidnap her?" He asked, his steel-coloured eyes still burned with rage.

"That won't-"

"What are you doing? Getting her drunk?" He asked and reached for the ale in Paula's hand.

"That's mine." She snapped protectively and pulled the mug out of reach.

Enos laughed, and his sage green eyes twinkled in admiration at her. Until his gaze landed back on Liam. "Look, obviously, this isn't the place to discuss what's happened today." He explained with a smug smile.

"Fine, then finish your drinks and I'll meet you outside," Liam snarled. He shot Paula another dirty look of suspicion before he headed back to his friends.

"You heard him, finish up," Enos stated with a playful smirk as he downed the rest of his ale.

Paula did as instructed, and the pair placed their empty mugs on the bar on their way out.

Chapter Eight:

Moments later, Liam emerged from the tavern, still wearing the same scowl from before.
"What is she blitzed now?" He growled. "Let's do this back at the house." He commanded as he walked through Paula's and Enos' joined hands and broke their grasp apart.

"I guess we don't need to hold hands anymore," Paula muttered with a sheepish smile, then jumped to follow Liam with Enos in tow.

The trio walked in silence until they got back to Enos' home. Where they assembled in the kitchen and Enos put the kettle on for a pot of tea.

"Why is she still here?" Liam growled, his steel-blue eyes narrowed in a glower at Paula. Which then shifted to Enos, who still puttered about the kitchen.

"They wouldn't let me-"

"No offence, princess, but I'm not interested in your sob story. I was talking to Enos." Liam snarled, his gaze darkened in threat.

"Hey, don't talk to her like that." He snapped. Enos glared at Liam as he approached the table and took a seat between Liam and Paula.

"I watched them turn her away myself." He explained as he watched Liam in analysis.

"So what, now you're keeping her as a pet?" He retorted with a scoff of disbelief.

"I am no one's pet," Paula snarled, her cheeks reddened in anger.

"You sure looked like it with-"

"Enough, she's been through enough and I won't stand for you insulting her." Enos cut in, his eyes bulged in rage.

"Boy, oh boy. Does she have you wrapped around her little finger, or what?" Liam chuckled with an amused smile. "They must be teaching something really special up there in-"

"I said enough," Enos growled and slammed his hand on the table. Before he could say more, the whistle of the teakettle interrupted, and he got up to attend to it.

Meanwhile, Liam and Paula locked eyes and remained in a tense, staring match until Enos returned.

"She's not one of them. They kidnapped her," Enos explained as he brought a few cups and the kettle to the table.

"What?" Liam asked, his scowl faltered as his gaze bounced between the pair of them.

"She was a…" Enos swallowed hard as he hesitated to say the rest.

"A prisoner." Paula's groggy voice interrupted, and a lump formed in her throat as her eyes met Enos' in realization.

"A prisoner with a silver spoon in her mouth," Liam mumbled begrudgingly, but his eyes held a semblance of remorse. Then he crossed his arms over her chest in a pout as he stared at the table in thought.

"Liam, enough." Enos snapped in a weak voice with a scowl at his friend, then his tender gaze returned on Paula.

"It's fine." She mumbled in a barely audible voice as she rose from the table and headed for the door. A weight settled in her chest and threatened to bring her to her knees.

"Where are you going?" Enos called after her as he got to his feet, too.

"I just need some air," she muttered. Her body tingled in the numbing feeling of shock.

"You shouldn't be out there alone," Enos stated as he took a few steps to follow.

"I'll be okay," she dismissed in a hollow voice.

"But-"

"Let her go, she won't go far and we need to talk," Liam interrupted with a dismissive wave.

Paula passed through the door and into the cool, dusky evening air. She stepped to the side and leaned against the cold, stone wall as she let out a long, guttural sigh. Then sank into a seated position

as she pressed her back even harder against Enos'
home.

Paula cupped her face in her hands as she sighed
again and tried to settle the anguish that threatened
to bubble up and bring her ale to the surface.

She'd stayed outside until night had fallen, and the
star above twinkled into existence above her.

"I was worried you might have run off," Liam stated
as he stepped out of the house and stood next to
her.

"Isn't that what you wanted?" Paula replied in a
groggy voice.

"Well, it didn't work, so I guess I should have chosen
a better tactic." He tried to tease, but even he knew
that was a poor choice.

They sat in strained silence for a moment as Paula
continued to appraise the sky in search of familiar
constellations.

"Look I'm sorry for-"

"Don't worry about it." She dismissed, "It's all in a
name and I wouldn't trust me either if I were you."
She explained, not bothering to look at him.

"What do you mean?" He asked and sank to the
ground to sit beside her.

"My silver spoon allotted me a fair amount of extra
time. I did a lot of reading. Your name means
protector, which is exactly what you're doing for
Enos." Paula stated with a sideways glance at him. "I
can't blame you for protecting the person you care
about most. I just wish I had someone like that." She

explained as her vision blurred and a pain radiated through her chest.

The corners of his mouth turned downward in a frown of sympathy as Liam placed a hand on her shoulder. "Well, now you do." He murmured and grunted to clear his throat in discomfort.

"What do you mean?" She asked through a tearful gaze.

"He means we're going to take you in and take care of you," Enos replied as he emerged from his home, then walked over and plopped down on the other side of her. He leaned his shoulder against hers affectionately.

"I don't-"

"You can't say you don't need us because we know you have no one else. Also, because you deserve better than to be dumped on the street and left to fend for yourself like Senator Marco did to you." He interrupted as he grabbed her hand in his.

"This is my cue to get out of here. I'm not doing any more of this mushy shit," Liam grumbled, then groaned as he got to his feet.

Enos laughed as his friend disappeared inside. "He's not the most subtle of people." He commented. The beginning of a smile of amusement tucked itself in the corner of his mouth.

"You don't say." Paula giggled in agreement.

"There's that smile I've been missing." He mused as his sage green eyes twinkled in adoration.

"Thank you," she murmured, and another smile crossed her lips.

"For?" He asked with a furrow in confusion.

"For caring. For being here for me all day and when I needed someone the most." She explained, her sandy-coloured eyes welled with tears of joy.

He reached up and wiped them away.
"I'm going to tell you a secret that I've been holding on to. One that even Liam didn't know until a few minutes ago." He stated. A nervous smile crossed his lips as he continued to appraise her. "Do you remember the story I told you about my neighbour?" He asked, his eyes glimmered with hope.

She nodded, unable to find words as her heart stilled in their tension-filled gaze.

"My neighbour's name was Paula." His voice faltered at the admittance.

Paula's jaw dropped as she stared at him and the realization dawned on her.
Recognition tickled the back of her mind as she and Enos continued to stare at one another.

His sage green eyes glistened at her in the moonlight and a young boy's voice echoed in the back of her mind.

"I'll always be here for you." She muttered in a zombie-like state as she blinked away the memory. Her gaze fell to his nose, and she reached out to tap it with her finger, in muscle memory. "Nose" she muttered. A part of her was unsure why she did that, but another part resurfaced in a feeling of reawakening.

"Hi, La." He mumbled as tears welled in his eyes and he pulled her into a tight hug.

The pair of them held each other and cried in relief for a long moment.

"I meant it when I said it all those years ago. I'll always be here for you." He mumbled into her neck and then pulled away to lay eyes on her again. "And now that I've found you again, I'm never going to let you go." He vowed, his Adam's apple bobbed as he swallowed down the emotions that threatened to continue spilling out.

"How did I forget?" She asked as she cupped his face in her hands and took in every detail.

"I'm not sure, but all that matters is that I have you back." He mumbled, then leaned in and their lips met in a tender embrace.

Paula froze in surprise before she sank into his gentle grasp as he pulled her closer. It finally felt like that missing piece she'd been longing for had clicked into place.

The End

Thank you for reading.

Acknowledgements:

First, I'd like to thank Mackenzie D for the idea behind this story. You introduced to ekphrastics, which is typically a poem or piece of writing inspired by a work of art. For these purposes, it's a piece of writing that's based on a particular image taken by me.
So thank you, friend, for the idea that led to this story.

Next, I would like to thank one of my favourite people, Alexander M., for always being willing to share your knowledge and willing to pitch in with the assist as needed.
You taught me what a palanquin is and I can't express how much I appreciate you for it! Thank you, Mr-Knower-Of-All-The-Things.

Thank you to Mark G, or Papa Mark, as I affectionately like to call him. For always giving me that little extra push to step it up and catching so so many grammatical errors.
As well as helping me in particular with those opening lines in the first chapter.

To Dharrsheena for helping me with the overall flow of the story. Thank you for lending your sharp eye to find repetitive language and sneaky typos!
Thank you, my friend!

To my feline friends and prickly pal, thank you for spending countless hours sitting at a desk and staring at a screen with me. Also, for your endless cuddles that you provided as I typed away at the computer.

To my husband, for being there to hash out the details of my stories, even if you have no idea what's going on. But also, for reminding me that love conquers all, even writers mania.
Thank you for loving me and showing the value of it to me. Once again, this one was for you.!

Lastly, to my readers, thank you for your support and encouragement!! Without you, my work would go to waste.

Thank you,
Donna Fox (HKB)